The Dance Fairies

For Caitlin Kennedy,
who's full of fairy magic

Special thanks to
Narinder Dhami

ORCHARD BOOKS
338 Euston Road, London NW1 3BH
Orchard Books Australia
Level 17/207 Kent Street, Sydney, NSW 2000
A Paperback Original

First published in 2007 by Orchard Books

HiT entertainment

A CIP catalogue record for this book is available
from the British Library.

ISBN 978 1 84616 497 2
9 10 8

Printed in Great Britain

Orchard Books is a division of Hachette Children's Books,
an Hachette UK company

www.hachette.co.uk

Imogen
the Ice Dance
Fairy

by Daisy Meadows

ORCHARD BOOKS

www.rainbowmagic.co.uk

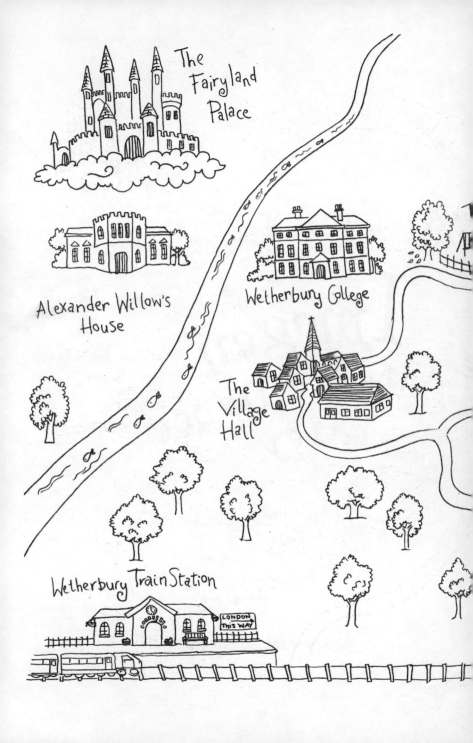

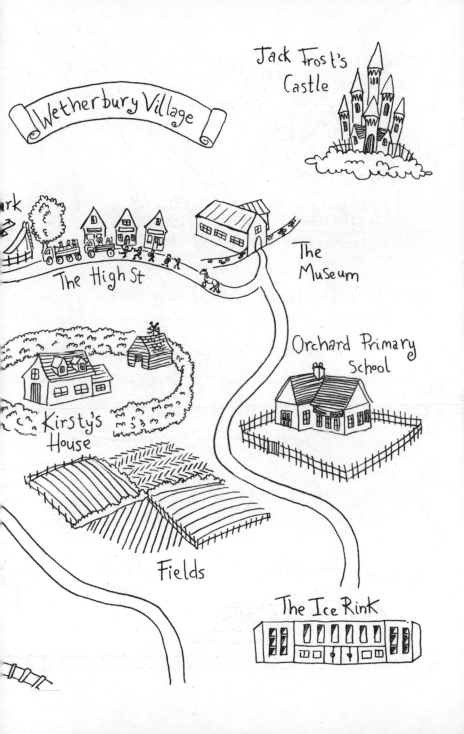

Hold tight to the ribbons, please.
You goblins now may feel a breeze.
I'm summoning a hurricane
To take the ribbons away again.

But, goblins, you'll be swept up too,
For I have work for you to do.
Guard each ribbon carefully,
By using this new power to freeze.

Contents

A Sparkling Skate

"I can't wait to see the show!" Kirsty Tate told her best friend, Rachel Walker, as Mrs Tate dropped the girls off outside the ice rink, promising to pick them up again after the show. "I love ice dancing!"

"So do I," Rachel agreed.

"Good afternoon, ladies and gentlemen!" A voice boomed over the loudspeakers as

the girls walked inside. "Welcome
to the Glacier Ice Rink. We have
a wonderful show for you today, so get
ready to see all your favourite fairytale
characters dancing on ice! The show
begins in twenty minutes."

There was a long line of people
waiting to hand over their tickets, so
the girls joined the queue.

"I wish I could ice dance," Rachel said longingly. "I can skate quite well, but I'd love to be able to do all those jumps and spins."

"Me too!" Kirsty laughed. "My friend Jenny's playing Sleeping Beauty in the show today, and she's a brilliant ice dancer! Let's go to the changing rooms and wish her luck before the show starts."

Rachel nodded but her expression was anxious. "With Imogen the Ice Dance Fairy's ribbon still missing, isn't Jenny's dancing going to be in danger?"

Kirsty nodded sadly.
The girls had spent
their half-term
holiday trying to
find the Dance
Fairies' seven magic
ribbons. Jack Frost

had stolen them so that he could use
their magic to make his clumsy goblin
servants dance properly. The magic of
the ribbons made sure that dance
performances everywhere, including
Fairyland, went well and were fun for
everyone. Without the ribbons, dancing
was ruined.

The King and Queen of Fairyland
had demanded that the magic ribbons
be returned to the Dance Fairies, but
Jack Frost had cast a spell that swept

seven of his goblins into the human world, each one clutching a ribbon to guard. The goblins were supposed to keep themselves and the ribbons hidden, but so far Rachel and Kirsty had managed to get six of the seven ribbons back.

"I'm just hoping the goblin with Imogen's ribbon turns up at the ice rink today," Kirsty whispered as they handed in their tickets. "After all, each ribbon is attracted to its own type of dance."

Rachel nodded. "I hope the goblin's here somewhere," she replied. "Mum and Dad are coming to take me home tomorrow, so we must find Imogen's ribbon before then."

The girls went into the auditorium where the ice rink was surrounded by rows of seats. Music was playing over the loudspeakers as people began to sit down.

"Let's go and see Jenny," said Kirsty, and she took Rachel over to the exit that led to the changing rooms.

As they entered the corridor, Rachel gave a gasp. She thought she'd just caught sight of something green disappearing round the corner at the end of the passage. *Could it have been a goblin?* she wondered.

"What's the matter, Rachel?" Kirsty called, as her friend ran down the hallway.

Rachel stopped at the corner, looking
this way and that, but
there was no sign
of any goblins.
"I thought I saw
a goblin run
round this
corner!" she
exclaimed, as
Kirsty joined her.
"But there's no one here."

"We've got goblins on the brain,"
Kirsty said, shaking her head. "Remember
what Queen Titania said – we have to
let the magic come to us!"

"Well, I hope it comes quickly,"
Rachel said with a sigh. "It would be
great if we could find the missing
ribbon before the show starts."

Kirsty and Rachel hurried to the changing room where Jenny and the other female skaters were getting ready. Jenny was in front of a mirror, pinning her hair up, when the girls came in. She smiled at them.

"Hi, Jenny," Kirsty said cheerfully. "This is my friend, Rachel. We've just come to wish you luck."

"You look great, Jenny," Rachel said, admiring her shimmering white dress.

"Thanks," Jenny said. Then her face fell. "I really want to do well today, but my Sleeping Beauty dance hasn't been going very well recently. I just can't get my moves right!" Kirsty and Rachel felt sorry for Jenny. They knew exactly why she wasn't dancing very well — it was because Imogen the Ice Dance Fairy's magic ribbon was missing.

"And I've just found out that there's an ice dancing coach coming to watch the show," Jenny went on. "If he thinks I'm good enough, he'll give me a place at the Ice Academy's summer school!"

She sighed. "I really want to go there, but if I don't skate well today, I won't get a place!"

Rachel and Kirsty glanced at each other in dismay. They had to find Imogen's magic ribbon before Jenny performed her Sleeping Beauty dance.

"We'd better get to our seats, Kirsty," Rachel said, spying the clock on the wall. "The show will be starting soon. Good luck, Jenny!"

"Yes, good luck!" Kirsty added.

"Thank you," Jenny said, pinning a white flower into her hair. "Kirsty, could you pass me my ice skates, please?" she asked. "They're in the corner, just beside you."

"Sure," Kirsty said, turning away to get the skates. She stooped to pick them up, and her heart skipped a beat; one of the skates was surrounded by a haze of blue sparkles.

As she picked up the shimmering skate, a tiny fairy zoomed out of it in a burst of sparks.

Kirsty recognised her immediately. "It's Imogen the Ice Dance Fairy!" she whispered in delight.

A Cupboardful of Trouble

Imogen hovered above the ice skate, waving up at Kirsty. She had long fair hair and she wore a beautiful blue dress embroidered with silver sparkles. Tiny white ice skates glittered on her feet.

Kirsty quickly looked over her shoulder. Rachel was still chatting to Jenny and the other ice dancers were

busy getting ready. Nobody had
noticed Imogen.

"Hi, Kirsty," Imogen whispered.
"I have good news. I can sense my
magic ribbon is very close by!"

"Really?" Kirsty asked. "Let's start
looking for it right away!"

"I was hoping you'd say that,"
Imogen replied with a wink. Then she
dived into Kirsty's pocket as Kirsty
picked up the other skate and took it
over to Jenny.

"Thanks," Jenny said, taking the
skates and beginning to pull them on.
"I wish I didn't feel so nervous!"

"Just do your best, Jenny," Kirsty said
comfortingly. "Rachel and I will be
cheering you on!"

Jenny nodded and
began lacing up her
pretty white boots
as the girls left.

"Poor Jenny!"
Rachel sighed as
they walked along.
"If only we could
help. But we don't
even know whether
the goblin with the
Ice Dance Ribbon is
actually around here."

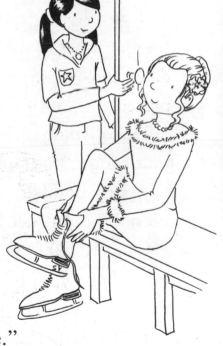

"Oh, yes, we do!" a silvery voice cried, and Imogen peeped out of Kirsty's pocket. Kirsty couldn't help giggling at the look of surprise on Rachel's face.

"Hello, Imogen," Rachel laughed. "So your magic ribbon is somewhere here?"

Imogen nodded. "We just have to find the goblin and get it back!"

"Oh!" Rachel exclaimed. "Kirsty, remember when I saw that flash of green on our way to see Jenny? Well, what if it was a goblin after all?"

"Let's go back and have another look," suggested Kirsty.

Quickly they hurried back to the corridor where Rachel thought she'd seen the goblin, and, this time, as soon as they turned the corner, they saw a goblin a little way ahead of them. He was standing outside a cupboard in the wall, pulling at the door handle.

"We've found him!" Kirsty whispered as they came to a halt. "But I can't see the magic ribbon!"

The goblin hadn't noticed the girls behind him, because he was too busy tugging on the door, but just then the door flew open so suddenly that the goblin fell over backwards. Looking a bit sheepish, he leapt to his feet and then plunged into the cupboard. The door slammed shut behind him. Rachel, Kirsty and Imogen rushed after him.

"Don't forget that while the goblin has the magic ribbon, he also has the power Jack Frost gave him to freeze things!" Imogen warned, as Rachel reached for the door handle.

The girls nodded. Then, quickly, Rachel yanked the door open and peered inside. Immediately, she gave a gasp of horror, because inside the cupboard she could see not one goblin, but seven!

Team Goblin

For a moment Rachel, Kirsty and
Imogen were too shocked to say
anything. All three of them stared at
the goblins who were busy pulling on
ice hockey kits of helmets, red jerseys,
elbow and knee pads and ice skates.

Suddenly one of the goblins looked up
and spotted the girls. He gave a screech

of rage. "Go away!" he shrieked.
"Don't you know it's rude to spy on
people who are getting dressed?" He
reached out to try and pull the door
closed, but Rachel held onto it firmly.

"Why are you putting on ice hockey
outfits?" Rachel asked.

"Don't you know anything?" another
goblin shouted back rudely. "These
aren't ice hockey outfits, they're ice
dance outfits!"

"Don't we look gorgeous?" said
a third goblin, and he began parading
proudly up and down the corridor.

"But they're not ice dance outfits,"
Rachel pointed out. "They're the kit for
an ice hockey team!"

The seven goblins looked taken aback
and glanced at each other in concern.

"Well, we don't care!" the biggest of
the goblins snapped at last. "We're
a team anyway – Team Goblin!"

"Yes, so go away and let us get dressed in peace!" shouted the first goblin and he tried to close the door again, but Rachel wouldn't let go.

"Listen, we'll leave you alone if you give us Imogen's magic ribbon!" she said, but the goblins ignored her and carried on dressing.

Kirsty scanned the cupboard and spotted a rather small goblin in the corner. He was struggling to put his helmet on with one hand, because, in his other hand, he held a sparkling blue ribbon.

"Look at that little goblin in the corner!" Kirsty whispered to her friends.

"He's got my ribbon!" Imogen declared, her eyes lighting up.

"How are we going to get it back?" Rachel asked urgently. "We need a plan!"

Just then the biggest goblin turned to the goblin with the ribbon. "I'll hold that ribbon for you, while you finish getting dressed," he offered with a sly smile.

"No, I'll hold it for you!" said another goblin, pushing the first one out of the way.

"Let me!" screeched a third, hopping awkwardly up and down in his skates. "I want to hold it!"

"No, me, me, me!" chorused the other goblins together.

"BE QUIET!" yelled the smallest goblin furiously. "NOBODY is going to hold the ribbon except ME!" He grinned smugly. "And now I'm off to dance on the ice!"

He dashed forwards, slid through Rachel's legs and ran off down the corridor. Before the girls could gather their wits, the other six goblins charged after him, knocking the girls aside.

"After him!" Imogen yelled, and the three friends gave chase.

The first goblin had danced his way along the corridor and was disappearing around the corner now. The others stumbled and tripped over their skates as they hurried after him.

"Come on!" Kirsty cried. "We have to stop the goblins getting onto the ice or everyone will see them!"

Slipping and Sliding

Kirsty, Rachel and Imogen rushed down the corridor after the goblins. But as they rounded the corner, and the ice rink swung into view, Kirsty's heart sank. She could see the smallest goblin zooming out onto the ice, waving the ribbon gleefully in one hand.

"This is awful!" Kirsty groaned, as the other goblins followed their friend out onto the rink. "Everyone's going to see the goblins now, and we still don't have the ribbon!"

"We mustn't let them out of our sight," Imogen whispered. "We might get a chance to grab the ribbon later." And she hid in Rachel's pocket, as the girls hurried to the edge of the rink.

The goblins were whooping with delight as they danced across the huge expanse of ice. As Rachel and Kirsty watched, they overheard a couple of women in the seats nearby, chatting to each other.

"I didn't know the junior ice hockey team was putting on a display today, did you?" the first woman asked. "That boy at the front is a brilliant skater!"

"Yes, but I thought the show was supposed to be about fairytales!" the other woman replied, looking puzzled.

"At least the audience hasn't realised they're goblins!" Kirsty whispered to Rachel in a relieved voice.

Music was still playing over the loudspeakers, and the small goblin with the ribbon began to dance in time to the beat. He glided expertly across the ice, performed a perfect pirouette and then launched into a series of spectacular jumps. The audience broke into loud applause. The other goblins, who were skating behind him in a long line, began trying to do the same moves. Rachel noticed that the goblin closest to the one with the ribbon managed to stay on his feet and even do some of the jumps, but the goblin at the end of the line could hardly stay upright, let alone dance. Rachel guessed it was because he was the furthest away from the ribbon and its dance magic.

Just then, the last goblin tried to jump
into the air but slipped and landed on
his bottom. He went skidding right
across the ice, knocking over the goblin
in front of him so that they both ended
up in a tangled heap. The audience
seemed to think it was part of the
show, and they laughed and cheered.

The goblin with the ribbon was still zooming around the rink, enjoying the applause. He lapped the last goblin in the line, just as he was struggling to his feet. The last goblin's eyes lit up as he spotted the ribbon flashing past him and he made a determined lunge for it. But the goblin with the ribbon dodged him easily, and veered sharply off the ice to run through the gate in the far side of the rink.

"Let's run round and see if we can head him off!" Kirsty suggested.

The girls shot off round the rink but by
the time they reached the other gate,
the last of the goblins had already
scrambled off the ice. He stuck his
tongue out at
Rachel and
Kirsty and
dashed off
after the
others, who
were clattering
down the hallway
in their skates.

"There's another rink at the end of this
corridor," Kirsty panted as the three
friends raced after the goblins. "I think
it's where the ice hockey team trains."

The girls sighed with frustration as they
saw the goblins pile onto the ice again.

This rink was smaller than the main one and had ice hockey nets at each end. Once on the ice, the goblin with the ribbon began to dance beautifully, leaping and spinning, while the others vainly tried to keep up with him.

"We need to get onto the ice and grab that ribbon!" Rachel said determinedly.

"For that, you'll need skates!" Imogen declared, and with a flick of her wand, the girls' shoes vanished and were replaced with snow-white skating boots.

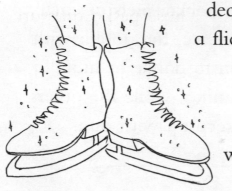

As the goblin with the ribbon glided around the rink, Rachel and Kirsty waited until he was near the gate where they stood, and then leapt out to try and snatch the ribbon away from him. Unfortunately, the goblin was too quick, so the girls had to skate swiftly after him, Imogen flying alongside. Just behind them were the other six goblins, still desperately trying to keep up with their friend.

"Look out!" shouted one of the pursuing goblins. "Those pesky girls are getting close!"

The goblin with the ribbon glanced over his shoulder and looked alarmed to see how close Rachel and Kirsty were. He sped up and started dodging from side to side, so that the girls couldn't grab hold of him. Rachel and Kirsty skated faster too, drawing away from the other goblins.

With the magic of the ribbon getting further away, the other goblins began to stumble and bump into each other. Suddenly, the goblin at the front of the line fell backwards with a loud shriek. He knocked into the goblin behind him, who bumped into the goblin behind him, and all the goblins went over, one by one, like a row of dominoes. They lay on the ice groaning and blaming each other.

"Stop fighting!" the goblin with the ribbon shouted, skating towards his friends. "We have to stick together to protect the ribbon from the pesky girls! Imagine how angry Jack Frost will be if we come back with no ribbons at all!"

The goblins stopped arguing at once.

"That's true!" one goblin said thoughtfully. "Those girls are sneaky. They dropped a moon on my head to get my ribbon!"

"Yes," agreed one with a very pointy nose, "They made me fall into a swimming pool!"

"Well, they bowled me down with a disco ball," another goblin said angrily.

"And now they're trying to take my ribbon!" the ribbon-holding goblin yelled.

All seven goblins glared at Rachel and Kirsty. "I think it's time to make girl popsicles!" the biggest goblin called, as they untangled themselves and staggered to their feet.

"Ooh, yes!" the goblin with the ribbon said excitedly, skating to a halt beside his friends. "I'd forgotten I could do that!"

"Watch out, girls!" Imogen cried.
"They're after us now!"

Rachel and Kirsty shot off across the
ice, as the seven goblins linked hands
and zoomed after them.

"We're right behind you!" the goblin
with the ribbon yelled.

"Freeze them! Freeze them!" the
other goblins chanted gleefully.

Rachel and Kirsty headed for the exit from the rink, but the goblins danced quickly over to block their path. The girls glanced at each other in desperation: they were trapped.

"Girls!" Imogen called, waving her wand over Rachel and Kirsty's heads. "Fly up to me!"

As the ribbon-holding goblin whizzed towards the girls, shouting "FREEEEEZE!" Rachel and Kirsty found themselves  surrounded by a cloud of blue fairy magic. Soon they were fairy-sized with delicate fairy wings. The girls zipped upwards to join Imogen.

"Come back!" the goblin yelled.
"I want to freeze you!" And he leapt
high into the air. Luckily, his
outstretched fingers just missed the girls.

"Please take your seats," a voice
announced over the loudspeaker. "The
show will start in three minutes."

"The show is about to begin!" Kirsty
gasped. "Jenny will be on the ice soon.
We must get the ribbon back!"

Girls Net Goblins

Rachel glanced around desperately, and her gaze fell on one of the hockey nets. "I've got an idea!" she exclaimed, pointing to the hockey goal. "Imogen, when I give you a signal, can you make that net tip over?"

Imogen nodded, then whirled off to position herself above the net.

"Follow me, Kirsty," Rachel whispered.

Kirsty nodded and grinned; she thought she had a pretty good idea what her friend was planning.

Rachel and Kirsty flew down and hovered low above the goblins, carefully keeping clear of the one with the ribbon.

"You can't catch me!" Rachel cried.

"Or me!" Kirsty added.

The goblins looked furious. All seven of them dashed forwards, desperately leaping into the air to try and grab Kirsty and Rachel.

The girls fluttered out of the goblins' reach, but remained close enough that the goblins kept trying to reach them. Little by little, the girls flew over to the hockey net where Imogen was waiting.

"Quick, Kirsty!" Rachel whispered. "Into the net!"

The two girls flew right into the net, and the goblins followed without hesitation.

"NOW, Imogen!" Rachel cried.

A cloud of sparkling fairy dust burst from Imogen's wand and made the net tip right over. It fell forward over the goblins, trapping them like a cage, but Rachel and Kirsty were small enough to flit through the netting and fly up to join Imogen.

"Let us go!" the goblins yelled
angrily, pushing and shoving
at the net. But there was no
way out. The net was too
heavy for them to lift.
Just then, Kirsty
caught a glimpse of
something blue
sparkling amongst
the tangle of
goblin arms and
legs. She flew
down, slipped her
hand through the
netting and pulled
the magic ribbon free.
Imogen clapped her
hands in delight as Kirsty
passed the ribbon back to her.

The fairy quickly reattached the ribbon to her wand and, as she did so, it shimmered a beautiful, deep blue. "My ribbon is safe at last!" Imogen sighed happily as the three of them flew over to the side of the rink. "All the Dance Fairies have their Dance Ribbons again, and it's thanks to you, girls. Now you must go and watch Jenny perform. I'll clear up here."

She waved her wand and Rachel and Kirsty were instantly back to their normal size again, and wearing their proper shoes. They watched as Imogen's magic then tilted the net

upright, freeing the goblins. They got to
their feet grumbling, and rubbing their
sore bottoms.

"Let's get out of here!" one mumbled,
and they began to skate off sulkily.
But without the magic of the ribbon
to help them, they kept slipping and
sliding everywhere.

"Stop!" Imogen called suddenly.
"You're not going anywhere with that
kit on!" And with
another wave of
her wand, the
ice hockey
outfits fell off
the goblins
and clattered
onto the ice.

The goblins scowled as they
scrambled off the ice without any
skates, complaining loudly about
their cold feet.

"Girls, I must go and give everyone
in Fairyland the good news!" Imogen
declared. "But don't worry, you'll see
the Dance Fairies again — maybe
sooner than you think!" She flicked her

wand and just had time to wave
goodbye before a shower of blue
sparkles whisked her off to Fairyland.

"We did it, Kirsty!" Rachel beamed as
they ran back to the main ice rink.
"We found all seven Dance Ribbons!"

Kirsty was smiling too. "Every kind
of dancing should go well again
now – including ice dance! Let's go
and cheer Jenny on!"

A Magical Performance

"Jenny's doing brilliantly!" Kirsty whispered to Rachel, as Jenny performed yet another amazing jump. She landed perfectly on the ice and then went into a fast spin. The audience clapped and Kirsty and Rachel joined in enthusiastically.

"She's great!" Rachel gasped as the music finished and Jenny took a bow.

Kirsty grinned. "At the interval, we should go and tell her that!" she suggested.

After watching Red Riding-Hood and the Wolf, followed by Cinderella and her Ugly Stepsisters, it was time for the interval and Rachel and Kirsty hurried off to see Jenny. They found her in the changing rooms, hanging up her skates.

"Oh, you'll never guess what just happened!" she exclaimed when she saw Rachel and Kirsty. "I've just been offered a place at the Ice Academy's summer school! They told me as soon as I came off the ice."

"I'm not surprised," Kirsty laughed as Jenny beamed at them. "You were fantastic!"

"And the whole show is going brilliantly!" Rachel said, smiling.

"Everyone seems to be skating much better today," Jenny said happily. "I'll come and watch the rest of the show with you when I've changed."

Rachel and Kirsty nodded and left the changing room to go back to their seats.

"I wonder what Imogen meant when she said we'd see the Dance Fairies again sooner than we might think," Rachel remarked thoughtfully, as Kirsty stopped at a vending machine to get a drink.

As Kirsty pressed the button, the machine began to shudder and shake. Then gold sparkles started whizzing around it.

"Fairy magic!" Rachel whispered, her
eyes wide.

As the girls watched in amazement,
a golden envelope fell
into the tray at the
bottom of the
machine, followed
by Kirsty's can of
drink. Kirsty
sprang forward,
put her hand
through the flap
and picked the
envelope up.

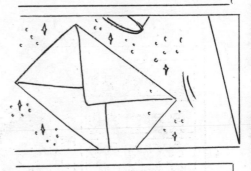

"It's got our names on
it!" she said in amazement.

"Open it!" Rachel urged.

As Kirsty opened the envelope,
a rainbow of bright colours burst from

it. Amidst the colours, a face began
to appear.

"It's Queen Titania!" Rachel gasped.

"And look," Kirsty laughed, "there
are the Dance Fairies, too!"

The Queen smiled as the Dance
Fairies fluttered around her, waving
happily at Rachel and Kirsty.

"Girls, once again you have helped us,"
she announced. "In return, we would
like to invite you to Fairyland for
a day of dance with the Dance Fairies."

"Ooh, we'd love to!" Rachel and
Kirsty chorused.

"Then we will come and get you very
soon, girls," the Queen laughed. "And
thank you!"

The Queen
and the
Dance Fairies
disappeared
in a
shimmering
burst of
colour, and
Kirsty and Rachel
gazed at each other in delight.

"I can't wait!" Rachel said, her eyes shining. "It's going to be fantastic learning all the different kinds of dance!"

Kirsty grinned. "We've had some great fairy adventures together, haven't we?" she said.

Rachel nodded. "And I've got a feeling that they won't be our last!" she said happily.

Win Rainbow Magic Goodies!

There are lots of Rainbow Magic fairies, and we want to know
which one is your favourite! Send us a picture of her and tell
us in thirty words why she is your favourite and why you like
Rainbow Magic books. Each month we will put the entries into
a draw and select one winner to receive a Rainbow Magic
Sparkly T-shirt and Goody Bag!

Send your entry on a postcard to Rainbow Magic Competition,
Orchard Books, 338 Euston Road, London NW1 3BH.
Australian readers should email: childrens.books@hachette.com.au
New Zealand readers should write to Rainbow Magic Competition,
4 Whetu Place, Mairangi Bay, Auckland NZ.
Don't forget to include your name and address.
Only one entry per child.

Good luck!

The Sporty Fairies

The Dance Fairies have got their
magic ribbons back. Now Rachel
and Kirsty must help

The Sporty Fairies

Starting with Helena
the Horseriding Fairy...

Magic Message

"There," Rachel Walker said, tidying her hair. "I'm ready. Are you?"

Kirsty Tate buttoned her jodhpurs and smiled at her best friend. "Yes," she said. "I can't wait!"

It was the first day of the Easter holidays, and Kirsty had come to stay with Rachel's family for a week. In a few minutes, they would be setting off for a riding lesson at the Tippington Stables, and both girls were looking forward to it. They always seemed to have the best fun when they were together – and the most exciting adventures.

Kirsty was just about to open the door, when something caught her eye. The pages of Rachel's diary were fluttering as it lay on her bed, and yet there was no breeze in the room. "Rachel!" she said, pointing. "Look!"

She and Rachel ran over excitedly. They had each been given matching bejewelled diaries by the King and Queen of Fairyland, as thank-you presents for helping the fairies. The two girls had been friends with the fairies long enough now to know that the fluttering pages of the book meant only one thing: something magical was about to happen!

Have you checked out the

RAINBOW
magic®

website at:
www.rainbowmagic.co.uk